The Toothbrus

by Justin Smith
art by Jamie Kan

ISBN

978-1-77302-001-3 (Softcover)

Published in Canada.

First Edition

"With my dragon appetite, I've got to keep these pearly whites."

"Or else my food will not go down,
my dragon throat to Tummy Town."

Dragons like to show their teeth, so brushing right is really neat!

**UP and DOWN, UP and DOWN,
once or twice and back around.**

"I brush, brush, brush after every meal, so eating sweets is no big deal

"Except for when I eat too much,
and my dragon teeth, they yell out 'OUCH'."

"My toothbrush takes good care of me, so I'll make sure it doesn't see.

"My teeth turn grey, or brown, or green
and fall right out in front of me."

"So as we dragons always say," 'Brush your teeth...'

When Tooth wakes up he likes to say...

"I'll brush my teeth the dragon way.

With my dragon appetite, I've got keep these pearly whites.

Or else my food will not go down my dragon throat to Tummy Town.

Dragons like to show their teeth, so brushing right is really neat.

UP and DOWN, UP and DOWN, once or twice and back around.

I brush, brush, brush after every meal, so eating sweets is no big deal.

Except for when I eat too much and my dragon teeth, they yell out 'OUCH!'

My toothbrush takes good care of me, so I'll make sure it doesn't see,

My teeth turn grey or brown or green and fall right out infront of me.

So as we dragons always say, 'Brush your teeth...

The dragon way!' "

— BY JUSTIN SMITH

CPSIA information can be obtained
at www.ICGtesting.com
Printed in the USA
LVOW01s0842100616

492067LV000 .B/2/P